Goodbye, Flicker

Goodbye, Flicker

Poems

Carmen Giménez Smith

University of Massachusetts Press

Amherst and Boston

LC 2012004386
ISBN 978-1-55849-949-2

Designed by Sally Nichols
Set in ITC Galliard
Printed and bound by Thomson-Shore, Inc.

Library of Congress Cataloging-in-Publication Data
Giménez Smith, Carmen, 1971–
Goodbye, Flicker : poems / Carmen Giménez Smith.
p. cm. — (Juniper Prize for Poetry)
ISBN 978-1-55849-949-2 (pbk. : alk. paper)
I. Title.
PS3607.I45215M36 2012
811'.6—dc23
                          2012004386

British Library Cataloguing in Publication data are available.

for Jackson, my son
and
Jorge, my brother

Contents

One

Two

Goodbye, Flicker

One,
in which she begins with pushpull.

⌢

We Shall Now Hear What Happened

Once   for a moment   once upon
once there was
there came   one day
a king   a tailor princess
the fisherman's wife
shepherdess   a girl   poor
lazy   clever   long and golden
hands like milk like silk stout and kind
true and faithful she floated
that she was
dreamt of   cross, clever
daughter of
wife to   sister witch   miller farmer tailor
very fine indeed good at heart
          in
tiny cottage   the larder   the edge
          the under   the in-between   and beyond
sister, mule, nanny   who loved her best
nightingale   swallow swineherd
who envied her who sent her to
that she became   in the deep deep   as she
had a   because she was to
to take   to draw   to find
left there
into   the deep deep
over   in the corner of
far inside
one day on an errand   to the seashore
the king's   to her nana's   for bread   left there
of
as promise   loss debt worry
at once   in the forest   on the path
pins needles   trees around her
sinister

stones roses   egg slipper basket teapot
farthings   a bottle of wine found and kept it
hid it   stole it
gave it away   an old crone   bitter   a stepmother
a sister mine   three things   three times
seven ways   four trolls   twelve sticks
and so   and so then   so then   a bone, a secret
the stone sang   a mouse   a mirror
a charm   gave her
later   counting   praying
and then   across the hills   riding horses
carrying a box   a shoe   a cloud
three wishes   one kiss   a last prayer
one cage   the song she'd sing all
she thought   she prayed   begged and reasoned
she saw   she cut

Owl Bits and Bits

The books she covets are labeled

with file folder labels she robs

from her father's desk. Owl builds a library

called *voluntad de oro,* which literally means,

Golden Desire or Golden Goodwill:

Gold for Wish or Wealth and Goodwill

for Desire or Love. The books were once

her grandmother's who had also lived

in the blue book and in the green book,

the leaves, the petals, the letters, the skins

in the books slip out and crumble like ash.

Those books told: her of north of the goose-girl,

of surviving caves and shipwrecks.

The words slip in and out like

the Wolf's tongue in Red's ear.

Backstory

the plot: an owl-faced girl with a loud family
engage in numbskull search
for deliverance from dreary sack of it.
a little something for the mind.

they try to cheap down food.
the specter of such drudgeries,
like housecoats and WIC,
too heavy, yet she, a pearl, a rarest thing.

the owl-faced girl's got her eye
on the curved security mirror.
makes her wide. she sees the unfolding

of the store. everyone slowly
in search. fingers brush against
cans. pause over shortcake

desire everywhere, so giant.
desire, a door in the security mirror,
rimmed in black, shadowy like a carny.

desire, her eyes flashed. she'd
go in but not in. leave and not leave.
no one would know, she reasoned.

the physical way? goosebumps. the soul way?
this one came from line of dreamers,
her mother: to marry paul anka.
her father: riches, no work.

blots out the obvious, scene by scene.
like whiting out. she vanishes
into her hands and *gets* vanished.

Hungry Office

Owl girl always bore shame for mother's brown
grease uniform. Mother told her
that entire cities really got managed
by cleaning ladies coming in night after night
to correct executive mishap in the moonlight.
Mops set aside for calculators, they formulate commerce.
The only lady to know European markets
writes her equations into contracts, seven-armed
document maker, the bedrock, floor by floor.
It was an ending like she likes: how maids feel
when they elbow through the vacuum dust
to distribute their wealth over miles of cyclone fence,
that their transport will come. All our mothers:
blank faces answering doors in movies.

If You Only Knew

why.
a cave that dripped
cold water. nothing
with a pink in it.

it was a thumbnail sketch
of the places no one went to.
why.
in the center of my chest,
a star of dull thudding.
my chewy center.
on some nights,
lead on my legs.
on other nights, a ghost

in my room. the vapors of dolls
choked me if I broke them.

avenues confused with talking
faces. I had a forked tongue.
a story to tell with one bit, and the way

to tell it with the other. I was unspooled
by the rancid perfection around me.
I had one leg. real glass eyes.

the sphinx question:
how else could one make it better?
the sphinx answer: with waiting.

What In Was

Easier as an alternative
to poke around the forest's theatrics
in books and in bones,
the saturation of wolves and elves,
witches and wishes. Dark and light.

In this one, she's got a magic needle and
sews up all the clothes she'd ever need
to look store-bought.

In this one she's got a key by the fire
made gold in her hand and she's
waiting on jordaches and polos,
husband and coin.

She's got a ring of crumbs
around her like bait. She grabs the walking
house by its heel and dips it in tar.

In this one her meager bones
carried through the village,
mocked, desecrated,
then lit by a mob.
Reinvention!

Stepsister

Wild girl of my nightmare,
the smell of morning patio
after all night wrestling bear-sized
infrequencies with no cigarettes
is what you are. My concrete boots,
my wet tomb. Regret is my new mode.
Princess, if you had loved me,
I wouldn't have co-opted your shadow
as mine. I cleaned you with sand
and daylight to keep you from fretful
and sullen. In the world for a long time,
we were each other's sugar dose
and marked the night with static
blips to pretend at sisterly fidelity.
I am still that fond lament.

Goblin School

Function: tyranny over gobbly sound.
Math and cursive? Hated both. The entire-
ty of my wholeness bubbled with their tedium.
When summoned for answers: kindle.

The resolve of the investigation tired,
so interruption was clippy or quiet
depending on the air tremors she smelled.
And numbers, what a sinister.
So that their imprint
wasn't glassy and sharp, she endeared
their game. The division of
the body is always two. *Why?*
Significance swells.

If the one that begins also adds,
then why begin there?
Class moved shiftily into
hierarchy of pencil boxes.
The inundation of monotone.
What context the bracket?

In school one day her bodies split
into a smell
from the ear. *Began to be*

was the smell of it. Flowerplus
and what a draft passed through
the middle. Not bothered—
split
like a ripe fruit no one sees.

Like fairies hear you, then hook you up
for which teacher said *daydream,*
said, *this one doomed. cashier or welfare.*

We were d&d squared.
The ones with wild hair.
Poor penmanship. Jheri curl envy.
Asthma sniffler.
Paper cut out. Fish-eyed face.
Hodgepodge grunts.
Bucktoothed riddle. Clammy wart.
Total transport was
the crib I was dropped into.
How far back can you
trace it? The nickels burn on her chest.
The huddle sparked.
Who was undoing her at this rate?
Sums and sums later. Still no answer.

"The Fates and Their Doors"

"The Poem of Mirrors"

"The Real Princess:"

"Delicate Sense of Feeling"

"Bugs Bunny Kisses the Saint Mary"

"World Three and the Dancing Sisters"

"The Forest Of Talking Appliances"

"The Fruit of a Thousand Kisses" or
"The Kiss of a Thousand Fruits"

"Swans In the Swan Orphanage"

"The Hermit, the Infant and the Bobbin"

"What Happened to You Inside of the Basket?
What Happened at Midnight in Deutschland?"

"The Flying Backwards Time"

"Other With Other"

"Interior Paint Troll and the Bridge of Unemployment"

"The Dragon: Pregnant With Possibility"

"The Coat and the Taxes"

"The Tale as a Screen Into the Kingdom and Nowhere"

"Afraid in the Mirror Said Thrice"

The Beast

The father told it so good
I wanted to carry the edges
of his robe, he and I.
We ruminated over thick books on
psychology and Japan and Marxism,
made his opinion aphorism,

turned personal affronts
into scripture, got derailed by visions
of golden paved roads
told just like I needed.

He invented my girlhood
and all
subsequent versions.

Psalms rose up and down in my chest
because they lived in the wispy hair of his head.
The clang of rage in early morning. Eureka.

His doctrine was the way a door
can know how it's opened or closed.
Truest dogma, the swindler's fabric.

Half-House

Medusa ringlets
and stone heart were
the ruin impulses
I bartered for my kindliness.
I bought land far off
for the ones who wander
off to dissolve them,
to disappear them.
I disguise the savor
of my hair as sweet,
make a house that
delivers greedy
to children's mouths.
I hide the bones, but
sometimes they win.
Children are just conceit.
My isolation,
now there's a theme.

The Prince

He was a metaphor for ineffable:
the other aspect of childhood wish.
She could not see him ideal.
Conceptual and faceless, he's
held aloft by the dancing birds
in the clearing, as in the facile iteration.

Theory Report

He was a long wait that deepened my fever
and begged me away from the window's
chasm, the chance
I had once been it.

First intended for, then lonely
with fidelity. Then the wonder whether
darkness had been the proof.
Or if echo.

The Poem of Mirrors

I climb through after folks kiss my forehead
and tuck Lulu, semaphoric princess of fuzz
and cherubity, into my arms, cover my scabbed
legs with nubby blanket.

they barely promise me the morning.
when they are gone, lights on me, the only
swishing fragility. the screen trills a heart tremor.
then it comes. treeline first. gallop and wind.

I'm

natasha on a black horse in the forest's
cloak. purple-brocade saddle.
away to the castle where the boy waits for

an important message on a scroll.
(*The king requests yer . . .*)
she's got a bird on her shoulder
to sing her into it.

she battles a *whatever* with a *something*.
then weakened, collapses into burly arms
that bring her to a canopied bed.
she lingers on edges of chamber music.
drifts. he never sleeps until her eyes.
and he says *please don't ever leave again*. she smiles.

large and rare and lots of gold.
big-faced purple flowers
would eat all the air if she let them.
horse whinnies under her window
so she throws a flower.

then, like that. it's morning
and lulu is on the carpet.
the ceiling's bumps line up
like little tiny letters.
and rising, rising,
I disappear like smoke until again.

Natasha's Chip

N: imagine me still inside this child. shut in her
piggish little body. a plastic fiddle from girlhood
thrumming mad because she's kept me here

on purpose. outside is still her dark cloud.
never mine. to keep me here: what good
when she gets it all. lookit: a real skin thing.

I'm saving up for my own place of bits and bits.
fragments of the stucco, what trees cast off, and
the joy over a ribbon she thought incidental

because she misnamed it. the whole world's gaze
upon her. that's the mortar.
a ghost lives better. I'm province of sublimation.

the same tomorrow. same old castle.
I'm divine though the light's been out for centuries.

Young Slave

Your leap is error, so the comb
in a box lined with glass?
Christen it artifact.
You'll die from it,
become the talking doll in the story.

A pall guards the door
from the human curiosities
in the room with heavy locks
where the glass layers always come off.

Treat her with cruelty,
says the voice, say all doors.
Then the mistress volunteers a name.
In this way, two are split needlessly.
October and November pass
like December and Owl Girl:
silent under it all.

What Out

rotten to corest is shadow to mother. is me.
mother feeds dreams to babies, changed
the ones that were weren't true true. like snow white.
wasn't cared for by dwarves. no prince.

snow's mother calls for her from inside the mirror.
no binding corset. the tower from
where the girl with the hair sings is two feet high.

the sleeping one wakes up to all kinds of abandon.
the children are deposited into the forest
only by deadbeat dad.

cinderella doesn't dance but sometimes in her chimney
sees out to the vista the pink and golden swirl
and remembers a lullaby saying *duerme duerme*.

so where will my days go?
always like this?

What Rage Was

My mother sits on the bed
with same story and closes her eyes
when the queen posts sentries

around the dwarf and *Dicho*!
mutters his name.
He explodes, but takes the queen's
como se dice. No one
knows except mother.
The king embraces her,
and she dissolves.

Someday my day will come
when she learns to say it right,
when she learns not to be all peasant,
just queen. For now,
she stumbles over it, leaves me
to this foreigner's world.

Thorny

I'm the doll in the highest turret
where I cast my mother into gnarls
and sire infants who consume
the last slivers of me. Head on a pillow,
I'm a saga drifting over the kingdom,
but this isn't why the place implodes.
The other explanation is my mother
combing the sycophant's hair.
My father? Gone too far on a boat
where he dispatches inquiries
about my disfigured face, makes a moat
into me, two points on a map.
A release of birds signals a grand mal
of fireworks because the prince
has come and touched my face.
Face: I mean mask.
Inquiry: I mean the awkward discourse
on the radio filled with misnomers
and allusions to battles with thorns.

Outside Source

Because, says the sliver poet,
the apple doesn't fall far from
refinery. the fragility of the girl.
the fragility of the mother.
one is a dangling
gold chain from the mother.
broken is as broken does.
because of panic. because
of the closing-in walls.

think for a moment,
says the sliver poet.
think of the protagonist's
round face in mother's hands.
saying what they say. think of
those wide open eyes
saying what they say.
think of a protagonist
catching a mother's
faraway eye glint.
the one that says: out
to lunch. snacking on a house
made of sugar and hay.
the shadows of expression
foresting her face are really
just deepest starving.
it is melancholy.
all our hungers
beneath the glow
of interior world.

Hans Hated Girls

On the beach and snapping
my suit free of the sand's dig,
I'm torch for the kelp,
for seagulls, for the one ancient
with hair who felt my legs
as a favor, he said. I don't settle
for voiceless. Don't settle for
legless and dropping
to the bottom like a clam, my soul
a bubble on the water's surface.
I'll see your hoax and raise it by five.
Yes, I'll stab the prince because
legs and voice are the same
things: exile out to in.

Refrain

What was quiet anyway?
Polluted with an interior noise,
not voice but static and whisper.
A pilot suffers noise fatigue from
the plane's benign hum,
sings over it to not crash.
No quality but insistence.

The shrieking of her
growing-up house subdues
with its buzzing quietude,
and when it died down,
everyone worn down from work,
from fighting, the house
still trembled with its own repugnance.

To Become an Exemplary Girl

I got wrapped in puppetry string,
the fingers that guide
and the flopping limbs doing
anything I can think.
Got wrapped and thought
I might become something bona fide.
I was a stir that dangled
and was dangled, made
stage exits wrong,
trapped inside and waiting
for the giant yawn
to release me.

Natasha's Got Hackles

natasha has a choice: boy or liberty.
he always cries when she chooses the horse.
he promises more than flowers.

natasha has a horse named Expectation
that sits outside. black horse
like night. doesn't smell like horse. more horseflower.

she goes always to the same ending.
goes there to come back sick. go, sick, OK.
the river stepped in twice is just movement so same.

Mother, Mother

my mother called snow white *blanca nieves.*
white snows. *white girl,* I thought. rain tick-marks

the window. *tick,* it says. *here is your time passing. tick tick.*
you grow old, it tells my mother. late for graveyard shift.

she tells of the mother. not a true one she offers
like a poor substitute, no. sweet'n lo packet of mothers.

she tells of apples that tempt because of the knot
of longing in blanca's stomach, a story about hungry.

she tells the part about blanca's collapse but the tick
mark is too urgent. to the denny's she must go. *more later*

or make the rest, she says. *I think you know what happens.*
yes. fading. a glass death. a kiss. the legacy mirror.

The Sliver Poet Returns

difference between this and dreams,
written by the sliver poet:
the quicksilver, the cynic, the poison.

the sliver signifies the shaft of light shed. that narrow.
sliver poet says: dream is conflation of self-holes in one story.
dream is the smudged page. dream is how shame is spilt.

if dream were more, then people would be better.
dream is a backdrop for waking life.

Q: I don't remember my dreams.
lie, says sliver poet. *dream is repetition of time with variation.*

Q: last night I dreamt that I kept my sister's head to my chest,
but a bullet killed all the same. for what good is that?
lie, says sliver poet. *nothing happens in dream. just finishing.*

Q: but.
A: *no.*
Q: if.
A: *hardly.*

sliver poet, listen. I woke with answers.
pause. *what type?*
mine.
lie. dream is not enough.
what can I know from it?
that you are a stop.

why?
because dreams go bad.
enrico-fermi-guarded-dreaming.

because it is a current when you can't see. language
is useless. what good is a chair if it dissipates?

what good is a mother
who wears such a foolish hat?
that's dreaming for you. take it if you'd like.

Bit Part

I was picked from the throngs
with nothing to show. They told me, *No, princess,*
you aren't dark enough for cinema, but
they forget that someone on the stage has to hoist up
the angels. Someone has to paint blood
on her wrists for the bathos.
In the next scene the star asks me
to kiss his mouth,
as if he had any gravitas.
My line speaks out of me
like a cartoon bubble.   *Illuminate me then burn me out!*
There's no pose in what I do;
I am negligible, I am pale.
My score is composed with broken glass.

Birds and Old Women

No one can live
that alone. I wasn't silent.
I fought with birds, old women,

brothers, cousins, sweaters. I built barricades
with blankets. *Who else could say what needed*
to be said? was what I thought. Shrill

and wild. Tear-streaked and angry. Once
I flew from the pull of a boat on a parasail,
saw down into the ocean and the little shivers wind

made over it. If the shivers got big and knocked
down the tourists, I could laugh—I wanted to be
the shiver so bad I was goosefleshed. Still do.

Unholy wish, to be bigger than the ocean, to knock it
about. But girl: that's what you is.

Two,
is the crawling out.

Post

The path to the deep wood
glittered with spring,
loose spangles of glow
pocked the grass,
and this light affixed to me.

He smelled like whistling,
the one who took down this story
so as I collected leaves
to touch into the veins of
this again and again that keeps
people at arm's length, I also
became the canopy of stone
I hide under when the rain—

This story was written onto
old book pages,
words marked over in black ink
could deliver cold or
the crosshatch of mathematics.
It felt intelligent to the nodding owls
silence had wrought from the forest
Words like a well, they said.

faeries, come take me out of this dull world. undo me from these harrowing
  serials.

unhand me from certain doom at the hands of my educators.

offer me elsewhere. take me back to the convex mirror. faeries,

I paid for mortification and will the audience know what to make of it?
  faeries,

my moral failings are best described outside of time: suspicion, greed, pride.

faeries, this renaissance of flesh confuses me. no one holds the key of me.

I'm living in illusion, relishing it, take counsel about complication from
  uncomplication.

faeries, draw down dark clouds upon my detractors. make me detractor like
  you.

faeries, let's shake the universe loose of filth and of deception and of
  betrayal. they have

physical names like beatrice and faeries, you have my fealty. faeries, I'll
  drink the potion.

I'll fall and fall. I'll go all odysseus on you and for you because what else is
  there but the other side of peter pan with a walker. wish on that.

Princess Madhouse

The institution was off a rural highway: buildings and rooms clinics
and a portable classroom. We were to heal through the mediation of
   professionals.
Some of us played dead and some of us played catharsis proscribed
roles given to us through diagnosis. Some of us were the rubbish
of kin carnival and we chewed on that spectacle in circles, and some
of us never got visitors. Some of us limned trauma onto
the soft spots of our legs with pens. We were the spiritual excess of
   glasnost. the realized versions of our parents' seventies capitalist
   experiments.

What Falling Was

(she falls into it)
I am so much to mar
was why
an old familiar hole, the sides
worn down from her own fingers,
those oils.
do you ever
get the feeling? the hole asked her.
like there's something you've got to do?

she fell and fell,
it was a lifeboat she was in. inside
she fell and fell.
the going unfamiliar, why it took
so long.

will she be okay?
who? no one was there.

Bluebeard

And how did he call owlgirl to his place?

With bugle and sugar.

And what were her charms and how much did they bring?

They were litheness and fallow, they brought fifty cents.

And why did the host voodoo-potion his guest?

For ascendance, for relish, for craven desire.

And when did she vanish under the tonic?

At noon and for always. This would be her derailment.

And where did the effervescence make her descent?

By the edge of his axe, in the sick pond of candle.

And what was the shadowplay etched on the wall?

A Punch and Judy fracas etched of clattering hips.

And who was left in the shadowy manse?

A sickening torque in her narrative, the theft of her late.

The River

the sliver poet's mouth has
an escape. form escapes as does
principality, which escapes
when she sleeps. she is cognizant.
the escape suggests
that when the girl is engaged
in her mind's escape,
well that something has got to be
guessed at with regards to—
with regards to escape.

slipping in and out so that the girl
barely notices her except
knows there's another side to it.
another read.
sliver's found some worn track out.
she said, *once it struck.* said,
this is where we come from,

mother earth, nature. she scooped up
the pebbly dirt from his turtle cage
for the eternities in them. what
a bother inside her. like natasha could

know, awoke too. descended upon
like pianos from windows.
focus for flint eyes.
pebble eyes. *drink water,* was urged.

potions, she muttered gutterly.
admonition meant what?

high, high. smelling requests
the sky made. wild and well-oiled
like sacred limb. gave over she was.

41

utter fits. all around the friends
consoled and cooed also altered.
I'm so good, gushed she. *so good.*

Where

natasha on a horse. natasha crying. natasha kissing.
natasha leaning on the castle's balustrade.
natasha writing songs on parchment. natasha fey.

natasha bony and weak. natasha fettered.
natasha bare. natasha flee. natasha of the gibbous moon.
see natasha. rest natasha.

natasha wet. natasha dettered. natasha equipped.
lithe natasha. craven natasha. natasha upon the pine tree.
natasha ill-fitting. natasha summers. joy-full natasha.

Into the Tower

You'd think I'd have noticed
but one never notices. Lip gloss
goes missing and I blame it on
poor memory. Mittens never gave it away,
always parted, but then a shoe.
By noticing I made it go faster like panic
in a movie when the camera swings
from right to left like it's the character's head
except it was me and my head swinging
back and forth, looking for my hair dryer,
my Joy Division record,

the bag I meant to put away.
I had long forgotten who I was,
had drowned under others' intimations of me.
My things made my shape.

I looked around but it was too late.
No one was left, not even the spider whose web
I was too lazy to get with the broom.
The web was still there so I went
for the broom, but it was gone. I knew this all along.

Pillows, the walls, the pictures of grandmother,
the day I couldn't escape myself
as an environment. I grew so hungry
for the dank, peeling cabbage rose wallpaper
that helped me feel populated, but I turned
inward until the world fell out
with my things. The quilt with the bloodstain.

The fountain pen
and its broken nib, the gloves
with powder in them,

44

my undergarments, the day's silt were secreted
away in the corners shaped like corners
then stored away in the cracks of my voice.

Academy

Dry kisses, bad eating habits, disgraceful
research, desire, the lack of a better word;
I blamed the imagination for all that went wrong.
My friends and I raced to become the most
prolific girl in school because we read sex books
from their mother's shelves. A teacher taught

us that theory might have something to tell us
about words and love. *This is real, yet it is not.*
I cut his class to dissolve a sliver of paper on my tongue
with friends who insisted on large and well-
experienced. I would have loved anybody. I did.

At night I served pizza to the trashy families
who left me their tips in dimes. I filled out
quizzes in magazines and sent letters to boys
who had gone away. I spit into your soup
when no one looked. So many mistakes,
and so little to show for them.

I made small nooks in the world,
then left them: empty nests,
unfilled hollows, gasps, yawns,
halls, doors, all things vacant.
Someone else might use them—I thought,
someone who knew better
what they were for.

Off

Take that hair out of your mouth,
paint it, shave your legs, look at boys all forlorn,
take their last names in a notebook
of curlicue, move along the hallways of school
with any sway you can muster, better yet,
get face from the TV.

I forgot I wanted to be tiny and grew ten feet tall.
It was a mistake to forget, for I was left out of
games I wanted like courtship and pageantry.
My mother reassured me only time, and sent
me into the woods where dusk happened.

I became a small colony in the world upon request,
a gauzy window into coy. I was hooded and set
loose with my colored face, so that someone might say,
hey that's new, uncharted and fresh. What I wanted:
a way from the careworn. My stories were tattered
rosary beads under my oily thumb. I could barely
fall in without falling out. I could barely fall.

Catastrophic Dreaming

Her bedroom is pubescent chinoiserie: thrift-shop silkslipper

and the ceramic madames all-parasoled. She was on the verge

of a massive unspindle, but would she be a pursuit

or the ritual of splitting the yolk from the white? She

detaches from the seducing marrow when vanishing is tremor

to very foundation that only she feels. Memorize this because

it's fablecloud. Rainbow or thorn or torch song or hopeface.

Sometimes she cultivates legitimate and other times, fantasy pasteling.

Her rough-hewn middleclass encroaches into her. The perimeters

of her father, the snowman, seeps into the carpet. If she could, she would.

Cocorococo, paloma. She separates the truth of harm from woods.

The dream of a china-pastoral clutters the shelf with its ladies.

Sliver Poet's Indictment

In your version we wander through blight
with waders on, up to our hips.
We squander minutes at peripheries.
Overhead we chant scorn until sense-like,
but don't blink for hours, don't go
to my happy place, don't write it down because
there's a doorframe around me,
and it's a lightning bolt with a cunning mole.
I call this Making Time For The Mercenary
and all you bring is, *I'm only tulle and you,*
shantung. Uncouth antagonist.
You're at the cleft scar below my kneecap
tracing and tracing again the moon.
Once we jittered like electrons, such orchestrated
straining. Once tenderness was our instrument.

Refrain Two

it was too much:
well enough said. how can
transport be too much?
suffice it to say you have a girl.
with so little meat to her,
figurative bones and
to trace around her,
leaves transport behind
but until then
it consoled. you would
be mad too. you would be
hurt if so unduly blessed
and cursed both.

and to see it. both blessed and cursed.
certainty is a trap. ingests truth.

Inside the Parabola

Inside the parabola
canopied by trees, and
reflecting back the light
in each character's eyes,
and the hand-sewn edges
of costume are exposed,
and when the animal chatter
dies away, the calming quality
of the arc vacates the tale,
or when you are teller,
the tale doesn't have a last part.

The Pulling of Butterfly Wings

Sliver poet says:
she will bear down on the stories. Watch her.
She will boil them into vapors
and breathe them to know them. It's part.

Her dissection will consist of a careful
consideration of each fairy's face while the first
wisps of cigarette smoke waft from her face.

It will be both sad and inevitable.

For the Potion

hated it. whored myself out for it.
shined the truth on it. vacated its premises
when asked, but then busted windows

in the complex. factory sealed it.
crescent mooned it. slacked into its corners
unmoored my dignity. made it gritty.

so like a limp. and the interior.
and the interior. and the interior.
what a vacate. except for natasha,

unslumbered and pissed. the fragments
of a stage with cobwebs. I would fruition
then leave it. I started you, didn't I?

Thumbkin

Made miniature by dint of powder,
owl girl is passed from palm to palm
but frets not, because to see the nicks
of a hand is a power: where vulnerable
lives. Unlucky in like, unlucky in
knowing, her mother's palm is red and
burnt, a wisp of powerless from it. Mum's
thumb drapes over thumbkin's little
body like animal skin. Made corpuscle,
smaller than thumb, than speck of dirt,
tinier than impulse. A cacophony
of surrender: bittersweet, that sleep.

And the Return

once in and remembering
not just being there but
what got me there.
no cobwebs,
just the fade of time.
the horse's face is *have we met?*

the horse's face is have we met,
and the castle's in the background
too like leaving wasn't wind
bearing down on her toothpick
house. she's feeling the walls.
around her and in too.
where. am. I, she barely says.
a smell like the inside
of the crook of her elbow.

got a light? she asks horse
because it's like that now.
the horse shifts into Light,
becomes part of shaft-

breaking tree canopy. *so movie,*
she complains.
the setting gets miffed.
someone waits at the castle.
she's got to come out herself.

chain the door. it's got to get said.
my first disaster glare-y and stiff.

like I'm going to tell you why
I am here. you tell. you figure it out.
you unwind

the strands of idea
from their spools.
this one

red for what? menstrual angst?
right. I was never
simple. red was for pride,
dummy. color association 101.

not so easy, perhaps, not so like this.
yet they find their way to it
since it's got a melody
that sings them into the river.

How Owl Girl decided to emigrate and the
consequences of her first attempt

The scabbard dragging behind her,
the occasional release from the old her.

Goodbye fear and hiding and pages.
She was living inside pages.

Her time is adrift and she's livid and imperceptible.
Ignored until she becomes imperceptible.

An occasional beau leaves behind the imprint
that gives away a cognition of paternal imprint.

Face to face, she's a sack of bones. she had perspective.
On the theme of emergence and for this perspective,

she would pay dearly. Having lived out of sense
to come back to earth, adopt some common sense.

The dénouement device is a fix to slake her thirst.
Appetite was an adrenaline cannon shot right out of it.

The Renegade Fairy at Beauty's Ball

Think on her rancor, how long-haired girls
got invited into the inner circle and not she.
She's raging presence and shivering absence,
a lagoon of extreme for her exclusion feels
folded into what she was, right in the center.

Sleeping beauty's narcosis was such a smart
scenario. The cocoon isolation releases her and us.

Problem is that renegade fairy shut herself in with a Joni
Mitchell lp and a sheaf of memories,
the instant replay of her moral outrage, with tenderness
and after the long exhalation
(iliveinaboxofpaints, amapofcanada),
remembered what recollections injure her.

The invitation squashed under the heft of her spell
book and old crushes most resonant like
the long-haired girls that reject her in
the angst-scored replays she made of their dealings.

Frog at the Moment of Impact

At the whim of both the father and the daughter,
the guest was forced to reevaluate his trajectory.
The effect of his feeling-thoughts: *I am the asshole.*

> (:and who's left in occupancy? the horse)

His smooth flight kept his audience well-mannered,
though sights of his mottled coat invited
a shout from the daughter's slim throat

> (sliver poet interjects with a plot
> advancing detail: *the intellect*
> *will win. rubbishy rubbish. this tale's about pragmatism*)

made hoarse by all her melodrama-weep, he thinks:
I pray the good you is coming. frog makes sense,
and to abate the hysteria, enforces the contractual detail.

> (*and troping it up with tarting it up? fie, author. she married*
> *him. desire plays no part in the thing*)

No comeuppance for our miss, the tale's failure.
Dicey, this curse business. His vengeance would
have been immutability, our schadenfreude.

True Events

And the father, once so broad-shouldered
finally living beneath such boulders. To get big
is to see the brittle quality of giants—
exquisite and queasy, those heights for me.
Doubt was my co-star, irony my flavor.
Traded me for my dumb, and these would be
the years called Rending Off
the Bone. The earth beneath our feet
spits lightning into the sky from
revelation such as: the infrequency
of family, the fading glow of elixir, that youth
can vanish as if by spell. This had been
the mother's curse and story. Hands gnarled
like gingerroot from clutching at paper towels
and I'm just finding my place in our place,
all that she wants. What narrow roads we're
offered and what enormous bales of Hope
on my back to carry through the village
in place of her, for her. Divided into bundles
for the whole nest of us, it's less than
something, more than nothing. But
to disengage, to fly off of to oneself as vocation . . .
such experiment. I can't find corresponding
choice in the mirror.

The Soft Landing

Harmony is one treasure she'll find.
Once she thought no one heard
her body break open like an egg,
her body hatching fantasy yet, so
changed, she glimmered like fool's
gold and everyone's seeing it. All
of her sleep's mutterings are clouds
that straddle her shoulder frame,
her beneficent skull. If held in too long,
secrets ring familiar in a family's quiet.
It's made right and impossible. The ghost
returns to us: blessed course to the district
of pillow, the borough of thorn.
So afraid of owing, she only tells the outline.

Natasha's Departure

What good is a story
without a heroine,
hobbled or not?
As we begin to end her
with a device, we give her
a claim to invention 'cos
she was a reflection back.
Tale's a screen for her
to step into and occupy.
Even reluctant, she's
queenish and flimsy
and then, *poof,*
the balloon let loose
into the atmosphere,
a neck that blossoms
into air: primary-
colored and curvine.

Tongue-Cut Sparrow

Sassy week and one day, the unsolved-her exploded.
The unexplored too. Part dos. All humanity was captive enthusiast.

I got her evolution—a dream of doing things
higher. If only we could be the patsy in the basket

who jumps out and shouts, *may diamonds and toads fall from
your mouth,* to the tyranny who runs away back home.

Glad I was maple in one. Got to sing top of it all. Survived
to see world open. Midnight and it felt nothing after.

Knees tread land-hard and semi-fulfilled and resenting.
I'm all dance in the room, a body torn up into pieces,

too silk, too force. Shit, I glowed *and* did
the windowing, looked in each fragment like light

through fog. *Docile girl,* I asked of the docile girl
left of me, *should I have buried my voicebox?*

The voice said, *be and bear and wonder the world.*
The world can bear & be too, even wedges without all of me.

No more dying then

I'll write mother a tale,
tell her the timid,
moody redbirds
still live in your hair,
and that the maps
carved into trees
are still in place
to guide her to
the house on legs,
the good one.

Tale is a world
of condition:
hazy stirrings,
nascent threats
in the air and
the cutup body
reconstructed by wish.

No more trap,
designated or fated.
No more dying inside,
figurative or real.
No more pathos.
The city would fill me.
The escape would revive me.

Notes

Many of these poems make reference to classic fairy tales adapted by Giambattista Basile, the Brothers Grimm, Charles Perrault, Madame de Beaumont, Hans Christian Andersen, and Joseph Jacobs.

"Faeries, come take me out of this dull world" is from the play *The Land of Heart's Desire* by William Butler Yeats.

The poem "Bluebeard" is for Brittany Chapman.

"Tongue-Cut Sparrow" is based on the Japanese folktale by the same title as adapted by Teresa Peirce Williston.

"Me for my dumb . . ." is a line from William Shakespeare's "Sonnet LXXXV"

The title "How Owl Girl decided to emigrate and the consequences of her first attempt" is adapted from a chapter title in the Jose Marmol novel, *Amalia*.

The title "No More Dying Then" is adapted from William Shakespeare's "Sonnet CXLVI."

Acknowledgments

Poems in this collection have appeared in the following publications:

"Theory Report" in *Brooklyn Rail;* "Bit Part" in *Coconut Poetry;* "To Become an Exemplary Girl" and "We Shall Now Hear What Happened" in *Fairy Tale Review;* "Stepsister" in *H_NGM_N;* "Mother, Mother," How Owl Girl decided to emigrate and the consequences of her first attempt," and "The Soft Landing" in *Lingerpost;* "Backstory," "Hungry Office," "Goblin School," The Poem of Mirrors," Natasha's Chip," "Outside Source," "Refrain," Natasha's Got Hackles," "The Sliver Poet Returns," "Where," and "If You Only Knew" in *Little Red Leaves;* "Bluebeard" in *Lumina;* "Sliver Poet's Indictment" in *Oranges & Sardines;* "Into the Tower" in *Palabra;* "Thorny" in *The Tusculum Review;* "Post" in *Xantippe.*

The
Juniper
Prize

This volume is the 35th recipient of
The Juniper Prize for Poetry presented annually
by the University of Massachusetts Press for a volume
of original poetry. The prize is named in honor of
Robert Francis (1901–1987), who lived for many years
at Fort Juniper, Amherst, Massachusetts.